WHAT ROSA BROUGHT

Written by Jacob Sager Weinstein

Illustrated by Eliza Wheeler

KATHERINE TEGEN BOOKS
An Imprint of HarperCollins Publishers

Katherine Tegen Books is an imprint of HarperCollins Publishers.

What Rosa Brought
Text copyright © 2023 by Jacob Sager Weinstein
Illustrations copyright © 2023 by Eliza Wheeler

Library of Congress Control Number: 2023933850
ISBN 978-0-06-305648-0

The artist used watercolors, ink, colored pencils, and block printing techniques to create the illustrations for this book.
Typography by Dana Fritts
Hand-lettered Yiddish on p. 30 by Gabriel Wolff
23 24 25 26 27   RTLO   10 9 8 7 6 5 4 3 2 1
First Edition

For Rosa's grandchildren: Simcha, Ben, Molly,
Simon, Erin, and Joe
—J.S.W.

For my bookmaking ally, Jen Rofé—
and for the memory of hers who lived it.
—E.W.

Rosa lived in Vienna.

Grandma looked after her during the day . . .

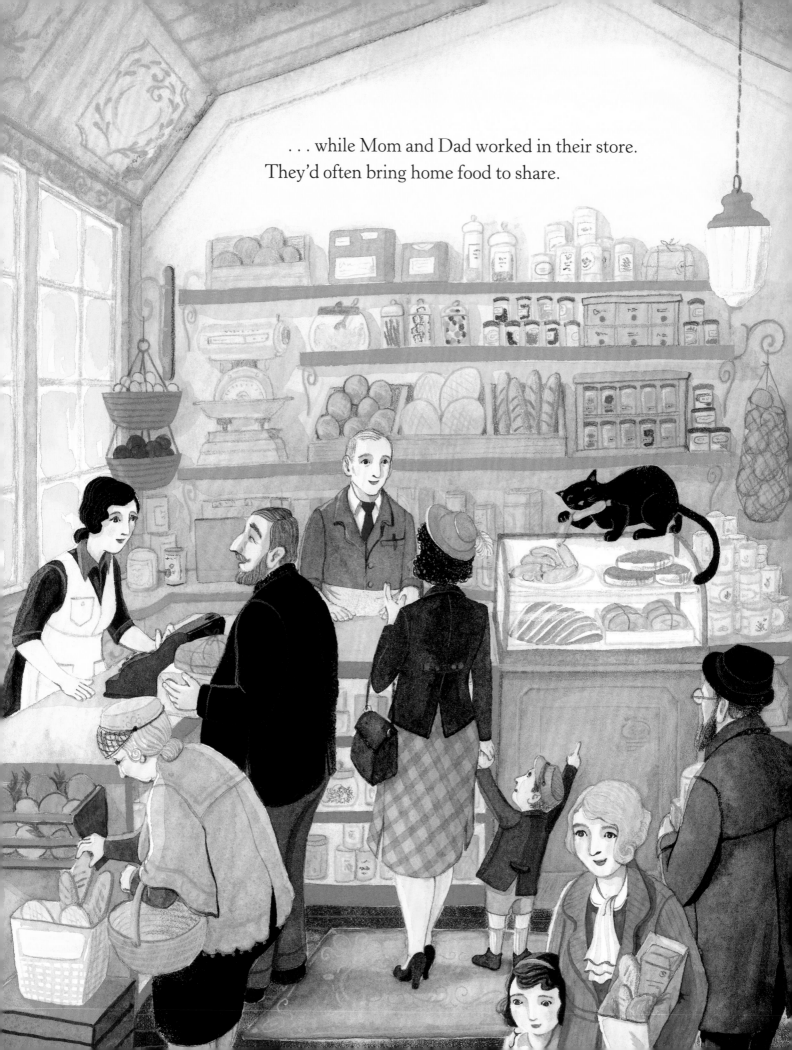

. . . while Mom and Dad worked in their store.
They'd often bring home food to share.

Their cat, Peter, would bring home food,
too, but he never shared it.

Then the Nazis came,

and things changed.

"What does that sign mean?" Rosa asked.

"It means the people who own that store don't want us in there because we're Jewish," Grandma said.

"Why does that matter?" Rosa asked.

"The Nazis say Jews are bad. Some people
believe them," Grandma said.

"Our customers are smarter than that," Mom said.

But Mom was wrong.

Soon, the Nazis made a new rule: Jewish people couldn't own stores or run businesses.

"Don't worry," Dad said. "Being a salesman isn't about what you carry on your shelves. It's about what you carry in your head. And I've got brains in mine."

Rosa read what Dad had written. "Don't you mean *trunks* for sale?" Rosa asked.

"That's the clever part," Dad said. "Selling *trunks* is a business. But selling one trunk? That's just a yard sale."

Secretly, Dad made lots of trunks. When someone bought one, he left the sign up, attracting another customer.

The Nazis didn't catch on.

The neighbors did. They heard hammering and sawing, and they watched people coming out with luggage. They could have told the Nazis about it . . .

But they never did.

If Dad bought wood, the Nazis might
see him and figure out what he was doing.
So he cut up the shelves in the grocery
store instead.

He was running out of shelves.

Many of Rosa's neighbors had disappeared—and so had Peter the cat. Mom and Dad said Peter must have run away.

"When will I see him again?" Rosa asked.

"I don't think he's coming back," Mom answered.

"Maybe he's gone to a place where he can have all the sausage he wants," Grandma said.

"Can't we run away, too?" Rosa asked.

"I have an uncle in America, and I hope we can go there," Mom said.

"Let's go right now!" Rosa said.

"America doesn't want to let us in," Grandma said. "We're strangers to them, and they're afraid we'll be lazy or make their country worse."

"Tell them we're good people!" Rosa said.
"Tell them we'll work hard!"
"I'll try," Dad said.

Rosa had finished her soup, but she was still hungry.
"What luck!" Grandma said. "You can help me finish mine."

Dad went to the embassy again and again, but they wouldn't give him a visa—the piece of paper that would grant them permission to enter America.

The Nazis still hadn't learned about Dad's trunk-making business, but other Jews had. One day, a rabbi came in with an unusual request.

"I have a visa," he said. "But I can't leave my synagogue's Torah behind."

"What's that?" Rosa asked.

"The Torah is a big scroll with the Bible written on it," Grandma said.

"Books teach us to think for ourselves," the rabbi said. "But people who think for themselves won't do what the Nazis tell them, so the Nazis have huge bonfires where they burn books. I will leave my synagogue. But the stories of our people and the laws we follow—these I will not let them burn."

Rosa wondered:

What would *she* bring with her if they left?

Her parents would want to take the one nice dress they had saved for her. It was white and hand pleated, but Rosa hated it. When she wore it, she couldn't play in the mud or climb trees.

Grandma would take an album of family photos.
Rosa often saw her looking at it.

Rosa decided she would take Peter's toy mouse.
He would want it when he found them again.

Soon, Dad had built a special trunk. "You can hide the Torah in here," Dad explained. "And then . . .

". . . it looks empty!"

The rabbi left Austria. And soon after . . .

. . . the family got their visa. "We helped the Torah escape," Dad said. "Now God is helping us."

But there was one problem.

"Why isn't Grandma coming?" Rosa asked.

"The Nazis say only three members of our family can leave," Grandma explained. "I'm the oldest, and you and your parents have many more years of life left than I do. It's right that you should go."

"I want you to come too,"
Rosa said.

"Even if I'm not there," Grandma said,
"you will take my love with you."

Rosa never saw her grandmother again.

But she took her love all the way to America and carried it in her heart throughout her life.

And that's what Rosa brought.

Author's Note

This is a true story, and Rosa grew up to be my mom. I don't know the exact words she and her family spoke to each other, so I've had to imagine them. I also imagined the moment where Rosa looked around her apartment in Vienna and wondered what she'd bring to America. (I didn't imagine the fancy white dress, though! My mom still remembers it unenthusiastically. You can see a photo of it below.)

Everything else is based on my mom's memories, the stories her parents told her, and whatever historical records I could find.

My mom arrived in America in 1939, a few days before her fourth birthday. As I write this, she's eighty-seven—older than her grandmother was when Rosa and her parents left Austria. And today, Rosa is a grandmother herself.

Rosa (in the white dress!) and her mother in America, 1941

Rosa with her parents and grandmother, 1935

My dad, Harris, me, and my mom at my
high school graduation, 1990

Rosa, Harris, and their granddaughter Erin, 2008